The Boy With Squar

Juliet & Charles Snape

SIMON AND SCHUSTER BOOKS FOR YOUNG READERS
Published by Simon & Schuster Inc., New York

SIMON AND SCHUSTER BOOKS FOR YOUNG READERS
Simon & Schuster Building
Rockefeller Center
1230 Avenue of the Americas
New York, New York, 10020

Printed in Italy by G. Canale & C.S.p.A. Turin

10 9 8 7 6 5 4 3 2 1
10 9 8 7 6 5 4 3 2 1 (pbk)

Library of Congress Cataloging-in-Publication Data

Snape, Juliet.
  The Boy with Square Eyes
  Summary: When Charlie's eyes turn square from watching television and everything else starts looking square too, he cures himself by reading books and stimulating his mind.
  [1. Television—Fiction.   2. Reading—Fiction]
I. Snape, Charles.   II. Title. PZ7.S66497Bo   1987
[Fic]   87-1293   ISBN 0-13-080524-6   0-671-69445-6 (pbk)

Charlie watched television all day long.

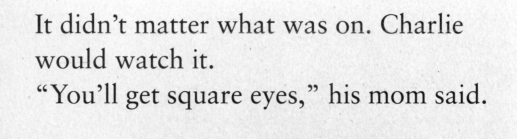

It didn't matter what was on. Charlie
would watch it.
"You'll get square eyes," his mom said.

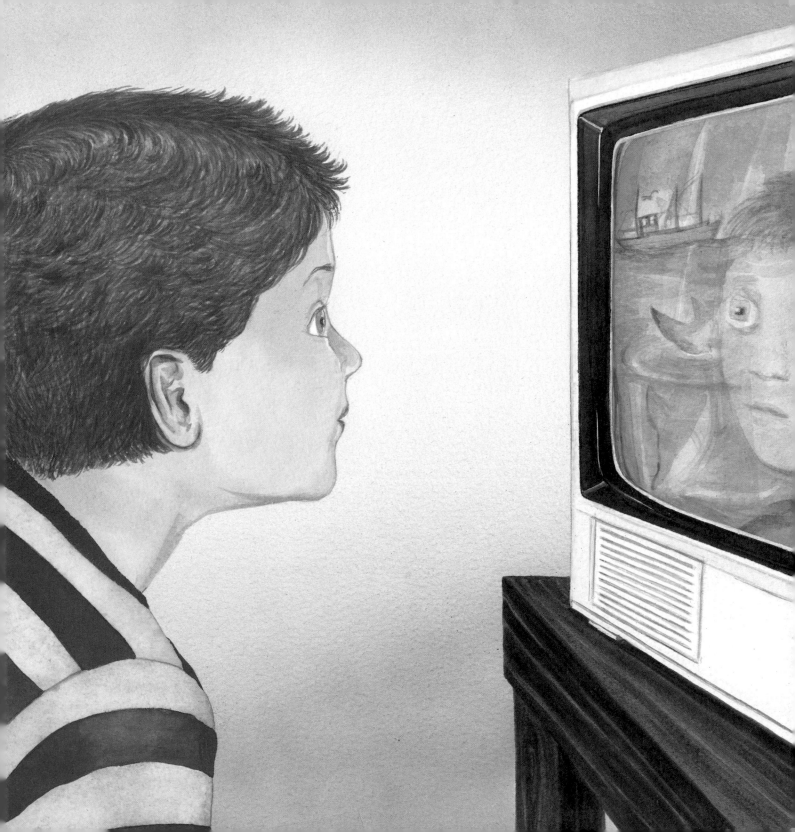

"Lunch," called Charlie's mom.
"Can I have mine in front of the
TV?" asked Charlie.
"No, come to the table."

Charlie went to the kitchen and sat down. "Mom," said Charlie, "the kitchen looks funny."

"Everything looks square," said Charlie.
"The food does too. Square plate, square
hot dogs, square french fries, square peas,
and square tomatoes."

Charlie's mom looked at the plate.
Then she looked at Charlie.
"Now you've done it!" she cried.
"Done what?" asked Charlie.
"You've gotten square eyes!"

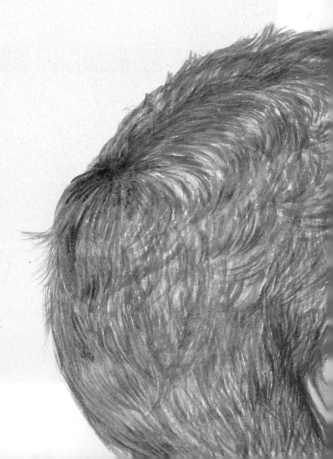

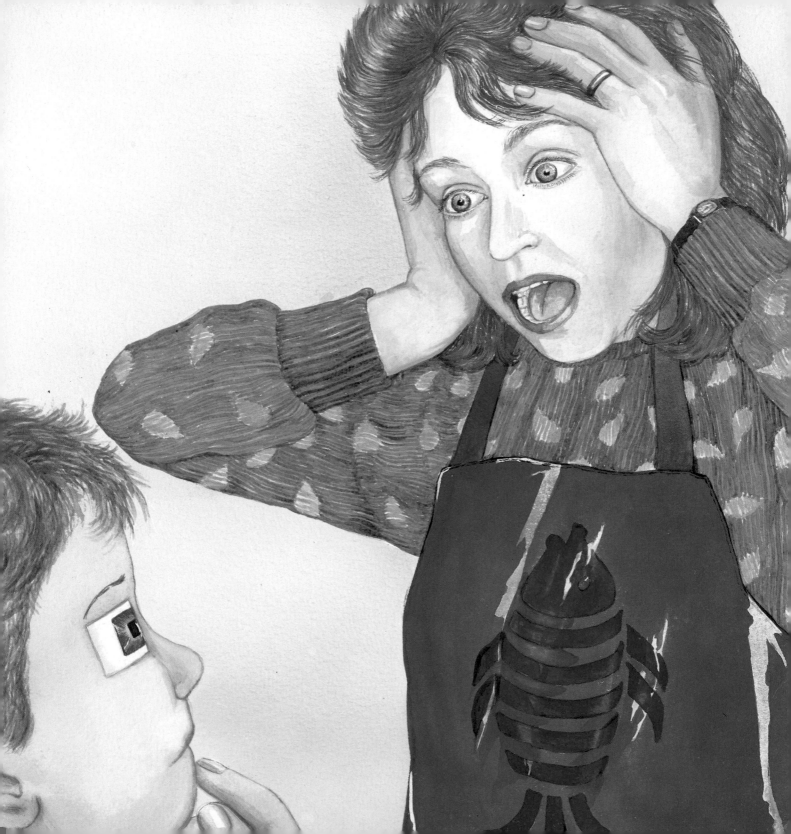

Charlie rushed to the bathroom.
"Mom! They ARE square! And so is
everything else."
"To the doctor!" said Charlie's mom.
"Let's hope she can straighten things out."
"But I don't need straightening out,"
said Charlie, "I need rounding out!"

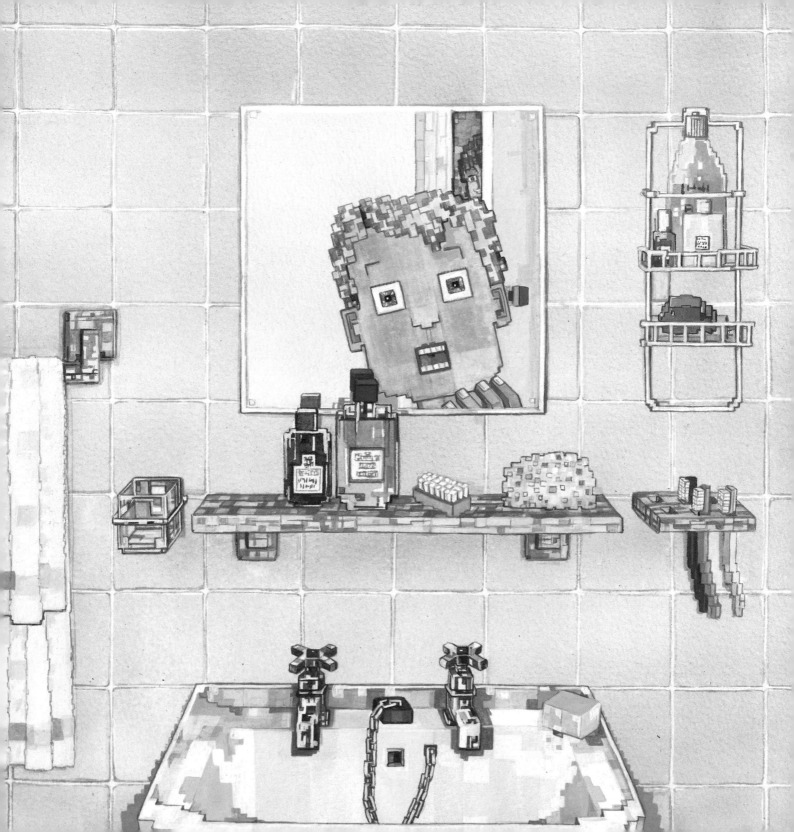

Charlie stared at the street as they waited
for the bus.
Things were just not looking right.

"Very odd, very peculiar," said the doctor.
"Very square!"
Charlie started to cry.
"Does he read books?" asked the doctor.
"No," said Charlie's mom.
"Does he go out and play?"
"No," said Charlie's mom.
"Does he draw pictures?"
"No," said Charlie's mom.
"Does he ever look up at the sky and wonder why?"
"No," said Charlie's mom. "He only watches television."
"Televisionitis," said the doctor.

"There is only one cure – to exercise your eyes."

They thanked the doctor and went out.

"The first thing we'll do is visit an art gallery.

Looking at pictures will help," said Mom.

"Well?" she asked, when they got there.

"I'm not sure," said Charlie.

Then they went to the library.
Charlie chose a few books.
"Any better?" Mom asked.
"A little," said Charlie.

After the library they went to the park.
Charlie looked at the trees and the birds.
Then Charlie's mom bought him a
hamburger.
"Feeling okay?" she asked.
"Mmm. . ." said Charlie.

When they got home Charlie's mom
unplugged the TV set.
"No more until those eyes are back to
normal," she said.
"Aww . . . Mom, I don't have anything to
do," Charlie said.
"Read a book, do a puzzle, draw a picture,
watch the goldfish, look at the sky."

So that is just what Charlie did.

He read a book.

He did a puzzle.

He drew a picture.

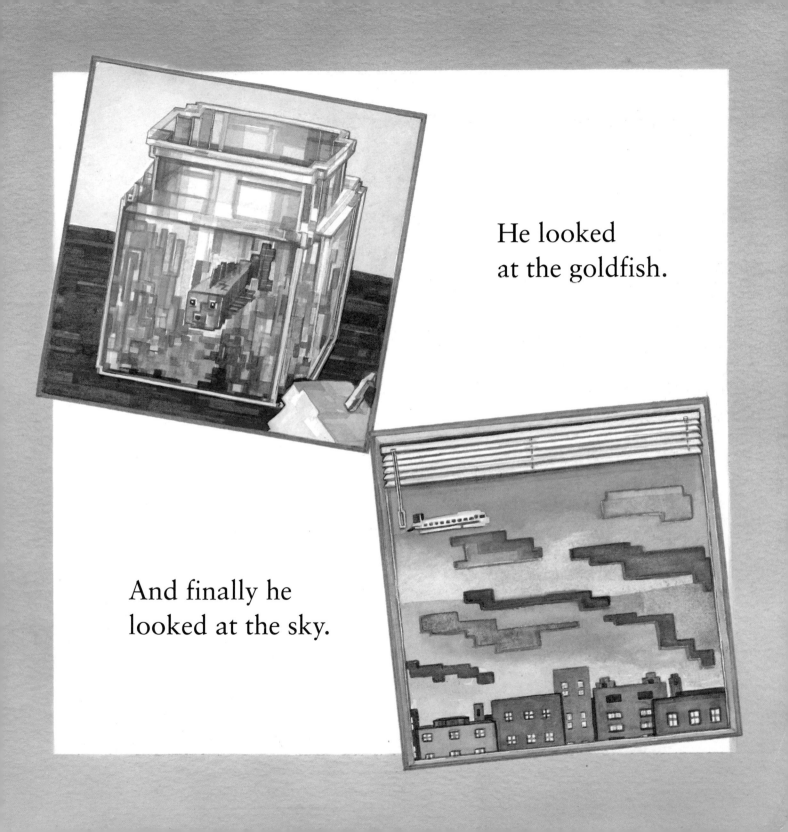

He looked
at the goldfish.

And finally he
looked at the sky.

Suddenly Charlie felt strange.
Questions began to come into his mind.
He just couldn't hold them inside any longer.
"Hey, Mom," he asked, "how far away is the moon?
What are clouds made of? How many people are in this city? Why does the world spin around?"
Charlie's mom rushed into the room.
"What's the matter with you?" she cried.
Then she stopped.
"Charlie! Your eyes! They're back to normal!"

"Great!" said Charlie.
But he never saw things quite the same way
again.